ARABIA

‖‖‖‖‖‖‖‖‖‖‖‖‖‖‖‖‖‖‖‖‖‖
✔ KU-349-815

THE GLASS PALACE
An Arabian Fairy Tale

and also
SLEEPING BEAUTY

by SAVIOUR PIROTTA
and ALAN MARKS

FRANKLIN WATTS
LONDON•SYDNEY

First published in 2004
by Franklin Watts
96 Leonard Street
London EC2A 4XD

Franklin Watts Australia
45-51 Huntley Street
Alexandria
NSW 2015

Text copyright © Saviour Pirotta 2004
Illustrations copyright © Alan Marks 2004

Editor: Rachel Cooke
Series design: Jonathan Hair

A CIP catalogue record for this book is available
from the British Library

ISBN: 0 7496 5433 3 (hbk)
         0 7496 5789 8 (pbk)

Printed in Singapore

Contents

Once upon a time

Sleeping Beauty is one of the most popular stories in the world and different versions of it can be found in many countries. In Europe, it was first made popular around 1636 by the Italian writer Gianbattista Basile. His tale was a big influence on the French writer Perrault and the German brothers Grimm who wrote their own versions. These two are now the most well-known.

Both these versions, and others told around the world, are full of symbols – images and events with hidden meanings. They are really about growing up, focusing on the scary process of changing from a child to an adult.

In *Sleeping Beauty*, retold at the end of this book from the tale by the brothers Grimm, the witch's curse is a symbol of the danger and pain that lurk through an adult's life. The king destroying all the spinning wheels in the land shows parents' attempts to shelter their children from the dangers of this world. But they cannot do this for ever. Inevitably, the princess finds the one spinning wheel left in the country. The story ends with a positive message: the princess survives the one hundred years and wakes up safe and sound – a grown-up ready to face her new life.

See if you can find any of these symbols in *The Glass Palace*. This story is from the Middle East and was first published as *The Ninth Captain's Tale* in *The Book of 1001 Nights*. Readers of *Sleeping Beauty* sometimes complain that the princess does nothing to stop what happens to her. The same cannot be said of Sittukhan, the heroine of *The Glass Palace*. Read it and see how she deals with the injustices that life throws at her.

The Glass Palace

In a distant city of golden minarets, there
once lived a young merchant's wife who
very much wanted a child. She had been
married for several years, but as hard as she
wished, the cradle by her bed remained
empty. Her friends gave her pitying looks
and her mother-in-law complained loudly
at every opportunity: 'When will I have a
grandchild?' In desperation, the young
woman went to see a powerful witch.

'Give me three bags of gold,' said the
enchantress, 'and I'll give you a daughter as
dazzling as the summer dawn.'

'Alas,' cried the merchant's wife, 'I do not have three bags of gold.'

'Give me two, then,' snapped the old woman. 'Your girl will not be perfect for such a price but men will find her as enchanting as a nightingale.'

'Alas,' said the merchant's wife, 'I do not have two bags of gold either.'

'Then give me one bag,' cried the witch. 'And the child shall only be pretty.'

'But I have only a handful of coins,'
sobbed the merchant's wife.

'For that,' sneered the greedy enchantress,
'your daughter shall be truly beautiful. But
she will have one small problem! If she so
much as touches a piece of cotton, she will
fall down dead.'

The young woman had no choice. She
paid the coins and left, praying the witch
would keep her word.

And so it seemed she did. Nine months later the merchant's wife gave birth to a girl, whom she called Sittukhan. She wrapped the child in linen and she and her husband made sure that not a scrap of cotton ever entered the house.

Their daughter grew up to be as beautiful and graceful as the enchantress had promised. The merchant's business had prospered, and now the parents dressed their precious child in the finest silk that money could buy.

One day Sittukhan
was sitting on the
balcony, feeding her
canaries, when a handsome
young man came by on a horse.
'Who are you?' he asked.
'My name is Sittukhan,' replied the girl,
smiling behind her veil.

Just then the
merchant's wife
called from inside.
'Come in from the
sun, my child.'

'I have to go,' said
Sittukhan.

'I shall come past your
house again next month,'
said the young man. 'Promise me
you will be here, waiting for me.'

'I promise,' said Sittukhan.

But the next morning she was again
feeding her canaries when an old beggar
knocked on the door to ask her mother for
water. 'Why does your daughter waste her
time looking after birds?' said the old crone.
'All girls her age should be embroidering
cotton sheets for their wedding chest. Why
don't you send her to the seamstress who'll
teach her to sew?'

Sittukhan overheard the conversation.
'What is cotton?' she asked her mother.
'Why have I never seen it or even heard
of it? And why do I not learn to sew like
other girls?'

The merchant's wife had no choice but to
tell her daughter all about the witch's
curse and why she had removed
every scrap of cotton from
the house.

Sittukhan did
not believe her.

'Pah! How could touching a piece of cloth kill you?' she laughed. 'The idiocies old people believe in!'

And after lunch, when her mother had fallen asleep, she slipped out of the house and asked the way to the seamstress's workshop. She drew her silk cloak around her and hurried through the streets.

At the workshop, Sittukhan sat on the
floor with the other pupils and watched the
seamstress work. How the needle seemed to
fly in her expert hands, diving in and out of
the material faster than the eye could see.

When the seamstress held up a robe she
was sewing for a caliph, everyone gasped.
It was embroidered all over with fish and

doves, and canaries just like the ones
Sittukhan had on her balcony.

'They look almost real,' said Sittukhan
and, before she knew it, she'd reached out
to stroke a canary. Alas, the moment
Sittukhan touched the cotton thread, the
world grew dark around her. Just as the
witch had predicted, she fell down dead!

Her mother and father were
inconsolable. They refused to
bury their beloved daughter
under the ground. Instead
they built her a glass palace,
in the middle of a secret lake
far from their city. There they
laid her to rest on an ivory
bed, in a chamber with her
favourite poems written in gold high on the
walls. All around the palace they planted a
garden, full of herbs and perfumed trees.

Now it so happened that the young man
who had spoken to Sittukhan was a prince.
When he passed by her house again a
month later and found her not there, he was
heartbroken. He instructed his wazir to find
out where she had gone. The servant asked
around the city and told his master all he
heard. 'Sire, she lies dead in a glass palace,
in the middle of a secret lake far away.'

The two men found the lake and rowed out to the palace. As he approached the door to Sittukhan's chamber, the prince said to the wazir, 'Wait out here for me while I pay my last respects. I shall not be long.'

He went in alone, and knelt by the bed. How beautiful Sittukhan looked in her silken robes. Her skin was still glowing, her hair still shone. The prince took her hand and kissed it over and over again.

'My beloved,' he sobbed. 'If only I had taken you away with me the first time I saw you, none of this would have happened.'

The prince was about to kiss Sittukhan's hand again when he noticed a fragment of cotton caught behind the nail on her thumb. It had got stuck there when Sittukhan touched the caliph's cloak. Gently, he drew it out.

All at once Sittukhan let out a sigh and
opened her eyes. 'Where am I?' she
whispered.

   'You are with me,' said the prince. He
kissed Sittukhan on the lips and she kissed
him back. The two of them stayed there,
gazing into each other's eyes, for forty days
and forty nights. At last the prince stirred
and said, 'My wazir must be getting hungry.
I'll take him back to the palace and return
for you with a golden litter.'

He left the chamber but, as he was
crossing the garden, he noticed a beautiful
rose swaying in the breeze.
'That flower reminds me of
Sittukhan's skin,' he said
to himself. And he
returned to the golden
room, where he admired
the velvety smoothness
of Sittukhan's skin for
another three days.

On the fourth day, he once again stood
up and, promising Sittukhan he would
return, left the room. This time he made it
as far as the gate at the end of the garden.
But, as he was opening the gate, a blackbird
flew out of the bushes. 'That bird reminds
me of Sittukhan's hair,' he said. And he
returned to her once more, where he sat
admiring the softness of her locks for
another three days.

At last the wazir called out and said,
'Sire, they will be getting worried about us
at the palace.'

'I am coming,' answered the prince.
He kissed Sittukhan one last time and left
the room.

'I wonder who he is talking to?' thought
Sittukhan. And tiptoeing
out of the chamber, she
followed the prince
down the marble
steps into the
garden.

The prince was closing the
gate when he noticed her
watching him through the
trees. 'You are not yet my wife,'
he cried, 'but already you spy on
me. You do not trust me, Sittukhan,
and so I shall not return for you.' And he
left without once looking back.

Halfway across the country
the prince had a change of
heart. How could I be so
cruel to someone who
loves me, he thought? And
he turned back to fetch
Sittukhan, but neither he
nor the wazir, could find
the secret lake again.

Meanwhile, Sittukhan wandered around the glass palace, sobbing with grief. How could someone who swore he loved her leave her for such a small mistake? 'I wasn't spying on him,' she cried. 'I only wanted to know who his friend was. Oh, I wish I was really dead.'

She was about to throw herself in the lake when she noticed something sparkling in the water. It was a golden ring, with a scarlet diamond on top. Sittukhan rubbed it against her arm to clean it.

In a flash of red smoke, a genie appeared in front of her. 'Speak, mortal,' he bellowed. 'Your wish is my command.'

'I desire a marble palace right next to that of the prince,' said Sittukhan.

'Shut your eyes,' ordered the genie.

Sittukhan obeyed and, when she opened her eyes again, she was standing in a marble palace. She called for her servants and they put on her face a silken veil hung around with golden coins.

Sittukhan leaned out of the window and, some time later, saw the prince returning home on his horse. The prince looked up and saw her too. He had no idea who she was but her beautiful eyes reminded him of Sittukhan, whom he missed very much.

When he reached his palace, the prince
called for his mother. 'Take the young
woman next door a gift,' he commanded.
'I want to marry her.'

That very same afternoon, the queen
presented herself to Sittukhan and gave her
a priceless rug. 'My son sends you a gift as
a token of his love,' she said. 'Take it and
accept his hand in marriage.'

Sittukhan thanked the prince's mother, then called one of her servants. 'Tear this rag up into floor cloths,' she ordered.

The servant obeyed, cutting the rug into pieces right in front of the queen.

'The girl must be so rich, your gift was an insult to her,' said the prince when his mother returned home. 'Take her something better.'

The queen went back to Sittukhan's palace with a jade necklace.

Once again, Sittukhan accepted the gift but called her servant. 'Throw these peas to the pigeons,' she ordered.

When the queen saw the servant scattering the beads in the garden, she said, 'What will my son have to do to prove his love for you?'

Sittukhan answered, 'If he truly loves me, let him be wrapped in seven shrouds of white linen. Then carry him through the streets in a black litter. At night, bring him to my garden where my servants will bury him alive in a marble tomb.'

The queen said to
the prince, 'Forget her.
Her price is too terrible
to pay.'

'I have already lost one
beloved,' said the prince, 'I shall
not make the same mistake twice.'
And right there and then he fell to the
floor and closed his eyes as if he were
dead. His body was wrapped in seven
sheets of linen and carried on a litter
through the streets of the city. His mother
followed the funeral procession, tearing her
shawl and wailing.

At night the prince was set down in Sittukhan's garden, outside the marble tomb. When the mourners had left, Sittukhan came out dressed as one of her servants, with her veil drawn across her face. She unwrapped the sheets one by one until the prince was free.

'You must be very much in love with my
mistress if you are willing to be buried alive
for her,' she said.

'I am,' said the prince.

'But how long will your love last this
time?' asked Sittukhan. 'How long will it be
before she makes a small mistake and you
throw her out?'

'I shall never leave her,' cried the prince. 'I have lost one I loved before and I never will again.'

'In that case,' said Sittukhan. 'I accept your hand in marriage.' And she removed her veil so that the prince might recognise her.

'It is you, my Sittukhan!' he cried. 'I shall never betray you again. I promise on my mother's heart.'

And he and Sittukhan remained there, gazing into each other's eyes for forty days and forty nights. And it is said that, when they got married, there was not a happier couple in all the world.

Sleeping Beauty

This version of Sleeping Beauty *was made famous by the brothers Grimm, who first published it in 1812. They called their story* Briar-rose, *the name of the sleeping princess. It appeared in their* Nursery and Household Tales, *a collection of folk stories the brothers had been told as they travelled around Germany.*

A long time ago there were a king and queen who had no children. But it happened that once, when the queen was bathing, a frog crept out of the water on to the land, and said to her, 'Your wish shall be fulfilled; soon you shall have a daughter.'
What the frog said came true and the queen had a little girl. The king could not contain himself for joy, and ordered a feast. He invited not only his relatives and friends, but also the wise women, so that they might give his child

magic gifts. There were thirteen of them in his kingdom, but, as he had only twelve golden plates, the eldest was left out.

At the feast the wise women bestowed their magic gifts upon the baby: one gave virtue, another beauty, a third riches, and so on, with everything in the world that she could wish for.

When eleven of them had made their promises, suddenly the thirteenth came in. She cried with a loud voice, 'The king's daughter shall in her fifteenth year prick herself with a spindle, and fall down dead.'

And, without saying a word more, she vanished.

Then the twelfth wise woman, whose good wish still remained unspoken, came forward and said, 'It shall not be death, but a deep sleep of a hundred years, into which the princess shall fall.'

The king, who was determined to keep his child safe, ordered every spindle in the kingdom to be burnt. Meanwhile the gifts of the wise women were fulfilled. The princess grew up to be beautiful, modest, good-natured and wise.

Now it happened that on the day when she was fifteen years old, the king and queen were not at home, and the princess was left to play on her own. So she went round looking into rooms she had not been in before.

At last she came to an old tower. Climbing up the narrow, winding staircase and reaching a little door, she opened it to find an old woman spinning flax in a room.

'Good day,' said the princess. 'What are you doing?'

'I am spinning,' said the old woman.

'What sort of thing is that, rattling round so merrily?' asked the girl, and she reached out for the spindle.

Scarcely had she touched it when she pricked her finger with its pointed end. All at once she fell down upon a bed and lay there in a deep sleep.

And this sleep extended over the whole castle: the king and queen, who had just come home, fell asleep and the whole of the court with them. The horses, too, went to sleep in the stable, the dogs in the yard, the pigeons upon the roof, the flies on the wall; even the fire that was flaming in the grate became quiet and slept and the roast meat left off frizzling. The cook, who was reaching for the scullery boy to box his ears, went to sleep. And the wind fell, and on the trees before the castle not a leaf moved again.

Round about the castle there began to grow a hedge of thorns, which every year became higher and thicker until it had covered it completely. But the story of the beautiful sleeping 'Briar-rose', for so the princess was named, went about the country, so that from time to time kings' sons came and tried to get through the thorny hedge into the castle.

They found it impossible, for the thorns held fast together, as if they had hands, and the youths were caught in them and died a miserable death.

After many years a king's son came again to that country, and heard an old man talking about the thorn-hedge, and that a castle was said to stand behind it in which a beautiful princess had been asleep for a hundred years.

By this time the hundred years had just
passed, and the day had come when
Briar-rose was to awake again.
When the king's son came
near to the thorn-hedge, it
was nothing but large and
beautiful flowers, which let
him pass unhurt. In the castle
he saw everyone and everything asleep,
even the cook in the kitchen with his hand
still out to seize the boy.

He went farther into the castle and came
to the tower stairs. He climbed them and
opened the door into the little room where
Briar-rose was sleeping. There she lay, so
beautiful that he could
not turn his eyes
away. He
stooped down
and gave her
a kiss.

In that instant, Briar-rose awoke, and looked lovingly at the king's son. The two went down stairs together as the king and queen awoke and with them the whole court.

The horses in the stable stood up and shook themselves; the hounds jumped up; the pigeons upon the roof pulled out their heads from under their wings; the flies on the wall crept again; the fire in the kitchen burned up and flickered; the joint began to frizzle again; and the cook gave the boy such a box on the ear that he screamed.

And then the marriage of the king's son with Briar-rose was celebrated with all splendour, and they lived contented to the end of their days.

Taking it further

Once you've read both stories in this book, there is lots more you can think and talk about. There's plenty to write about, too.

• For starters, think about what is the same and what is different about the two stories. Talk about these with other people. Which story do you prefer and why?

• Imagine you were organising a christening or a naming ceremony for a relative. Make a detailed guest list. Who would you invite to the feast and who would you leave out? Why?

• Rewrite one of the stories in a modern setting, perhaps placing yourself in the main role. How would your plot differ from the old ones, and why? Would your princess behave in the same way as Sittukhan or Briar-rose?

• Draw up plans for Sittukhan's and Briar-rose's palaces. How would they be different? You need to think about the materials used, the furniture, decorations and even the garden design.